A Very Fuddles Christmas

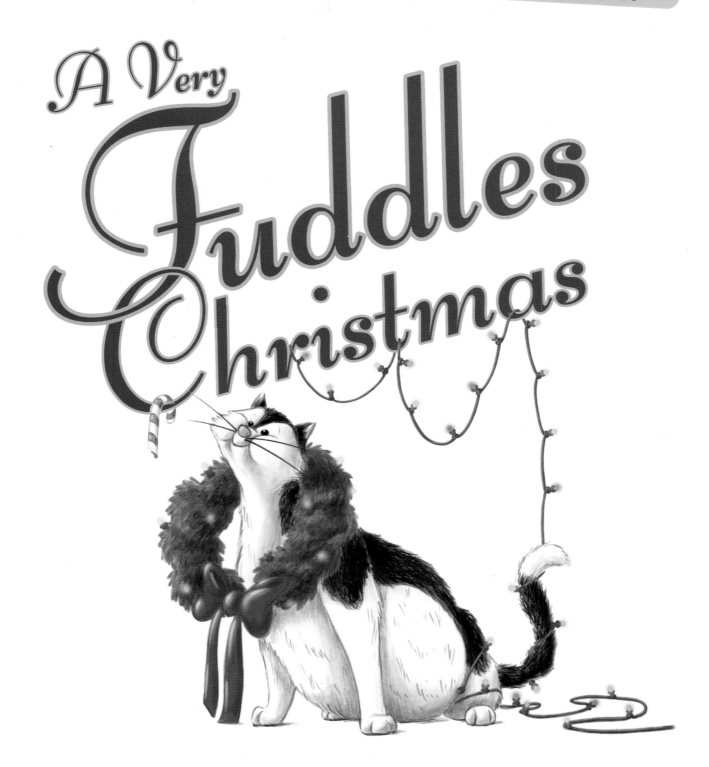

I want to thank my parents, Toine and Dorothy Vischer,
for letting me follow my dreams
• • •
Many thanks to the Karens at Aladdin:
Karen Nagel, Karina Granda, and Karin Paprocki

ALADDIN

An imprint of Simon & Schuster Children's Publishing Division • 1230 Avenue of the Americas, New York, NY 10020
First Aladdin paperback edition September 2018
Copyright © 2013 by Frans Vischer
Also available in an Aladdin hardcover edition.
All rights reserved, including the right of reproduction in whole or in part in any form.
ALADDIN and related logo are registered trademarks of Simon & Schuster, Inc.
For information about special discounts for bulk purchases, please contact Simon & Schuster Special Sales
at 1-866-506-1949 or business@simonandschuster.com.
The Simon & Schuster Speakers Bureau can bring authors to your live event. For more information or to book an event
contact the Simon & Schuster Speakers Bureau at 1-866-248-3049 or visit our website at www.simonspeakers.com.
Designed by Karina Granda
The text of this book was set in Wade Sans Light.
The illustrations for this book were rendered digitally.
Manufactured in China 0518 SCP
2 4 6 8 10 9 7 5 3 1
The Library of Congress has cataloged the hardcover edition as follows:
"'Twas the holiday season of treasures and treats. But Fuddles the cat only wanted to eat . . . And open his presents,
then sit down and play. But that's not what happened on one Christmas Day." —From publisher's description.
Subjects: Cats—Juvenile fiction. Christmas stories.
Genre: Fiction. Juvenile works.
LC classification: PZ7.V822 Ver 2013
LCCN: 2013404588
ISBN 9781416991564 (hc) | ISBN 9781534433571 (pbk) | ISBN 9781442435117 (eBook)

A Very Fuddles Christmas

WRITTEN AND ILLUSTRATED BY Frans Vischer

Aladdin

NEW YORK   LONDON   TORONTO   SYDNEY   NEW DELHI

Fuddles was a fat, pampered cat.

His family spoiled him endlessly.

One day, a yummy aroma
awakened Fuddles from his catnap.
What's that? he wondered.

He followed his nose into the dining room.

Me-wow!
Look at the delicious meal
his family made—just for him!

Fuddles was about to dig in, when . . .

"No, Fuddles! That's not for you!"

He dashed into the living room, where he found
toys and treats——just for him!

"Fuddles,
don't touch!"

"Stay away!"

"Be careful!"

But then Fuddles saw
the best gift of all.
A tree!
A tree with
twinkling lights and
glittering stars—
just for him . . .

to climb!

o - o - o - o - o - o - o!"

Fuddles ran as fast as he could.
Before he knew it, he was . . .

Outside!

He looked around in amazement.

What *was* all this white stuff?

What happened to the green grass and leaves?

Where were all the flowers?

And *brrrrrrrr* . . . . . it was cold!
Very cold.

Fuddles had to get
back inside, but now
the door was closed.

He called his family,
but they didn't hear him
or see him.

Maybe the back door was open.

Like a pioneer frontiersman, Fuddles
bravely faced the elements . . .

through the bitter cold
and biting wind . . .

ignoring his icy whiskers, frozen paws, and rumbling tummy.

Where *was* that door?

Danger lurked everywhere.

Plop!

Splat!

Ow!

Who did that?

Fuddles looked up and spotted squirrels! Pesky squirrels.

They had no idea what he was made of, did they?

Fuddles hopped and flopped.
He slid and skidded and slipped.

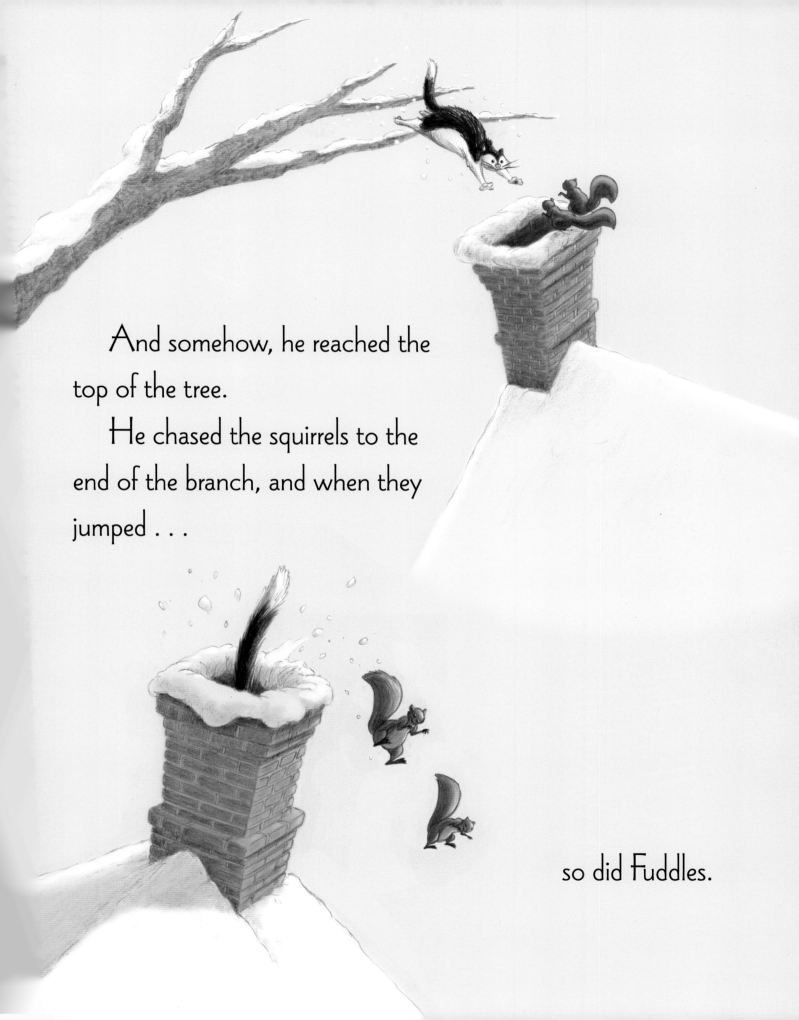

And somehow, he reached the top of the tree.

He chased the squirrels to the end of the branch, and when they jumped . . .

so did Fuddles.

And scary.

Uh-oh!
It was dark.

And smelly.

And dirty.

OOMPH!

"Fuddles! Where have you been?"
asked Mom. "Just be glad we didn't light
the fireplace yet."

A warm bath . . .

a soft towel . . .

a sweet scent . . .

and a home-cooked meal——

just for him.

Merry Christmas, Fuddles!